Meme McDonald & Boori Monty Pryor

flytrap

ALLEN&UNWIN

First published in 2002

Allen & Unwin
83 Alexander Street
Crows Nest NSW 2065
Australia
Phone: (61 2) 8425 0100
Fax: (61 2) 9906 2218
Email: info@allenandunwin.com
Web: www.allenandunwin.com

A Cataloguing-in-Publication entry is available from
the National Library of Australia
www.trove.nla.gov.au
ISBN 978 1 86508 608 8

Cover and text photographs by Meme McDonald
Cover design by Ruth Grüner
Paintings of The Binggaldamba and The Two Yams by Lillian Fourmile
Drawings of the flytrap and blowflies by Harry Todd
Photographs on pages 39 & 42 by Boori Pryor
Designed and typeset by Ruth Grüner
Printed and bound in Australia by the SOS Print + Media Group.

The paper in this book is FSC® certified.
FSC® promotes environmentally responsible,
socially beneficial and economically viable
management of the world's forests.

MIX
Paper from
responsible sources
FSC® C011217
www.fsc.org

20 19 18 17 16

For Grace

for being in our lives

And for our mothers

M.M. & B.M.P.

Nancy is worried. She walks out of the
school yard holding her mother's hand tight.
Her mum hurries on ahead with a million
things on her mind, as usual.

Nancy's worried. They drive home.
Her mum's busy with the traffic.

Nancy's worried. Her mum races up the
front steps of their house, rushes to the
telephone, presses the play button on the
answering machine, slices an apple, boots up
the computer, spreads butter on the fresh
bread . . . listening to the phone messages
and cutting vegemite fingers . . . types in a
password, warms the milk, logs on to the
internet, stirring the mug of Milo very fast.

Nancy eats her afternoon tea alone.
Worried.

At school, Nancy's class is learning about plants.

A few days ago, Nancy's teacher, Miss Susan, asked if anyone knew what a Venus Flytrap was.

Nancy's hand shot up. 'It's a plant that eats flies.'

'Very good, Nancy.' Miss Susan smiled back and Nancy felt as if the sun had risen over the horizon just to shine on her.

'Does anyone have a Venus Flytrap at home?'

Nancy watched, her sunflower-face lifted towards her teacher. Miss Susan was searching the room for someone extra special. With a mind of its own, Nancy's hand shot straight up again. Again, Miss Susan's sunny smile shone down on her, just her.

'Could you bring it in to show the rest of the class, Nancy?'

The whole class looked across at her.

Nancy nodded, trying not to explode into a million billion trillion beams of light. She felt very special.

Each morning, for three days in a row, Nancy told Miss Susan she was very sorry but she'd forgotten to bring her Venus Flytrap to school. Each afternoon she promised to bring it the next day.

This afternoon, before school finished, Miss Susan wrote a note in red pen on the back of Nancy's hand—V F T.

'Don't forget!' said Miss Susan, the shadow of a cloud drifting across one corner of her bright shiny face.

The school bell rang.

Nancy raced out to find her mum.

She was very worried.

The truth is—she doesn't have a Venus Flytrap!

Nancy can't hold on any longer. A big bubble-gum of worry balloons out ready to burst, to stick all over someone, or just blow up in her face.

'Mum? What am I going to do?' Tears bank up behind her eyes.

'Mmmmmm.' Her mum doesn't hear very well when she's checking her email, or surfing the net, or pegging out the clothes, or making dinner.

Nancy tries again. And again. Finally she gets through.

'It wasn't really a lie,' Nancy pleads. 'It was more like . . . a wish.'

Her mum doesn't rouse Nancy that much for telling a fib. She's the best mum in the world really, Nancy thinks. Or the busiest!

'Well, maybe you could say the rabbit ate it?' her mum says vaguely, tapping away at the keyboard.

Nancy rolls her eyes towards the sky. On the other hand, she thinks, sometimes my mum doesn't understand even the simplest things.

'Everyone knows that rabbits don't eat Venus Flytraps, Maarm!'

Her mum checks her watch and sighs. It's too late to rush down to the nursery to buy one.

'There's nothing I can do, Nancy.'

Nancy hates that brick-wall voice her mum gets when she's being pestered.

'The shops are shut. That's that.'

Tears spurt out in all directions, surprising even Nancy with their force.

'I can't go to school,' she shrieks. 'I can't face Miss Susan.'

Her mum keeps typing, her jaw clenched tight. Nancy's really pushing it now. Finally her mum takes a deep breath in.

'Maybe . . .' She looks up. 'Maybe you could tell your teacher that the cat from next door fell off the roof outside your bedroom window and dropped down hitting the icy-pole stick that was poking out on the ledge under your Venus Flytrap and the Venus Flytrap went hurtling up into the air and flew over the rooftops and went whizzing through the neighbour's kitchen window six doors down and landed in Hughie Robertson's bowl of cereal just when he was eating his Coco Pops and complaining they needed more sugar.'

A laugh slips out, making little cracks in
the solid cement of Nancy's worried face.

'Maaarm! Miss Susan's not going to believe
that!' she giggles.

Nancy loves it when her mum gets silly just
when Nancy has given up all hope and it feels
to her like the world has come to an end.

She's pretty good at making up stories,
Nancy thinks. For a mum.

'I don't know,' her mum says, turning back
to the computer. 'You make one up then, while
I finish this.'

Nancy lies on the floor, staring at the cracks in the ceiling, worrying.

'Maybe . . . maybe I can't bring my Venus Flytrap to school because . . . it got sick! It ate so many big fat blowflies it got a stomach-ache and vomited. I know . . . I know. It was Gee's smelly echidna that brought all these flies swarming into our back yard . . . and . . .'

Her mum groans.

Got her, Nancy thinks, sitting up. Trapped!

One mention of the smelly echidna and her mum gets in a state. She can't concentrate on her work. She *has* to stop and listen.

Gee is Nancy's step-dad. She calls him 'One-two-three, step-dad Gee' but that's because his real name is Garth. She'd never heard of anyone called Garth, so she named him her Gee.

Gee brought a dead echidna home two weeks ago. He'd been driving back from Lakes Entrance. He's really good at spotting things on the side of roads. 'Road kills,' he calls them. 'Poor little fullas,' he says. 'It's a waste to leave them lying there.'

He brings all kinds of things home in plastic bags. Mainly birds. Together, he and Nancy clean them up and lay the wings out like fans, pressing them flat under a pile of telephone books till they set. Greens and purples and reds and oranges of parrot wings; patterned browns and blacks of the wise old owls, and of eagles that soar overhead; whites and yellows of the loud cockatoos. They're all treasures to Nancy, each one with a story to tell.

**Nancy's mum held her nose when Gee
opened the boot.** 'This one's a bit funky!'

Sometimes mum's a real wuss, Nancy
thought, as she lifted out the dead echidna.

Gee's mum, Nanna, makes beautiful
necklaces with echidna quills. She puts a red
seed in between each one and strings them
together with fishing line. She's good at fishing
too.

Nancy hoped she might have a necklace all
of her own one day soon.

Gee phoned Nanna to ask how to get the
quills out.

'Boil 'im up first,' Nanna said in her quiet
way. 'Boil 'im up real good. Long time.'

Gee listened carefully.

'You got one of those hardware shops down there?' Nanna hadn't been to their house in the big city.

'Yes we have,' he answered, winking at Nancy.

'Then you go down to that shop there and buy up one of those pliers. You know, pliers?'

'Pliers?' Gee sounded surprised.

Nancy was too.

'Pliers?'

'Pliers,' Nanna said patiently. 'You pull those echidna quills out with that pair of pliers.'

'Really?' Gee chuckled. He was expecting Nanna to explain how to rub the echidna on hard rocks, or bury it in the ground for six months—something a bit more traditional than pulling them out with a pair of pliers from the local hardware shop.

Out in the back yard they built a fire. Nancy helped collect the sticks. They cleared around the fireplace so no dead leaves or grasses could catch alight. Gee showed her how to start the fire carefully, holding the flame away from the wind, so she didn't burn herself.

'Fire can be dangerous. A bit like echidnas walking on roads. You gotta watch out for things that can get you. Otherwise you end up as someone's necklace before you know it.'

Nancy got the hose and filled the pot with water. They put the dead echidna in, the lid on, and sat back.

Gee and Nancy yarned in the shade, stoking the fire. Gee reckoned 'echidna' was a word from some other language, like Spanish. In his family, the name for echidna is binggaldamba, but there could be five or six hundred different names for echidna, there

are that many languages across the whole
of Australia. And that's not even counting
porcupine or hedgehog.

'You know how he got them?'

'Got what?'

'Quills.'

'Nup.' Nancy felt the tingle of a story
coming on.

'The story goes . . .' Her Gee always has time for a story. 'Long time ago this one fulla was really greedy. He wanted everything for himself. He didn't want to share nothing. In our lore it's important that you share things. Not this fulla, but. He wanted to keep everything for himself. He used to go out hunting, catch a big lot of food, bring it back, eat it all up and then lie in the water, big and fat.

'Those other fullas, they got real angry with him. He wasn't satisfied with not sharing what *he* had. He also used to steal what *they* had!

'One day, they'd all had enough. As he was lying in the water thinking about his next feed and what he could steal, the other fullas picked up their spears and started throwing them at him. He rolled over and tried to swim away, but all those spears stuck in his back.

25 trap

As he crawled up on the land, he looked like a walking pin-cushion. He didn't know which way he was going.

'That echidna still don't know where he's going. He gets lost all the time, like this one here. He got lost and now he has to give up all his quills and end up round someone's neck as one of my mum's deadly necklaces, strung together with beautiful red seeds.'

The flames were leaping, coals were glowing, the pot was boiling. Nancy was quiet, listening.

'You got a lot of work ahead of you to make one of those beautiful necklaces. Those red seeds don't just drop out of the sky. When Nanna picks them, she gets them when the skins have turned black. She peels back the pod, and checks what colour the seeds are.

If they're pale, she's got to wait till they turn yellow, then orange, then red. As soon as they turn red, she drills a hole in one corner. If she leaves it too long and they turn bright red and shrink, they're too hard to drill and she can't make no beads. You see, that's where the story of the yams comes in.'

Nancy poked some more sticks into the fire, feeding the flames, hoping for another story. She'd learnt not to pester Gee but wait till he was ready to tell her.

Gee lifted the echidna out and left it to cool.

Later, they worked side by side, Gee picking the quills out with the pliers, and Nancy cleaning and laying them in the sun to dry. The quills were as sharp as spears. She packed each one carefully into a container with a tight lid, ready for Gee to take up north to Nanna.

Nancy couldn't hold on. 'Can you tell me that story about the yams now?' she pestered.

'Later.' Gee wouldn't budge. 'You have to wait for that one.'

The quills were safely tucked in his bag for Nanna when Gee caught the plane.

The rest of the echidna, though, was still out in the back yard. Gee was good at telling stories. He wasn't extra good at cleaning up.

Days went by. The echidna started to smell. By the time Nancy's mum noticed, it was covered in flies and she swore she wasn't going to touch it.

'That's One-two-three's business to clean up,' she grumbled.

'And . . . so . . . that's what happened to my **Venus Flytrap!** It got greedy and pigged-out on blowflies and got so full that it vomited and couldn't go to school.' Nancy watches her mum, waiting for a response.

Nancy's mum stays staring at the computer screen.

Nancy doesn't give up, making her brand-newest-bestest excuse for Miss Susan even bigger and better.

'You see, the flies smelt the echidna and came swarming . . . and . . .'

'Yuck!' Her mum looks up. 'That smell was so bad, wasn't it?' She can't help giggling. 'They probably smelt it from across the other side of Melbourne!'

'Further!' Nancy squeals, clapping her hands, thrilled that she's lured her mum away from the computer again. The sound of her mum's laughter is as sweet as a raspberry spider on a hot day. Nancy drinks it in. 'Flies flew for days to get here . . . from . . . maybe from . . .'

Nancy's mum squirms, remembering the feeling of flies squatting on the back of her sweat-soaked shirt, in the corner of her eye, up her nose, on the edge of her mouth, sucking the moisture.

The feeling of flies carries Nancy's mum back to when she was a kid mustering sheep. She grew up way out in the bush, miles from any town or city. It was flat and dry and dusty out there. The flies got so thirsty they'd settle on anything wet.

Nancy's mum swivels her chair around. Nancy wriggles closer, loving that when-I-was-little look creeping across her mum's face.

fly **31** trap

She starts to tell Nancy about shearing time and the sharp spiky blades, the smell of engine oil and warm wool, and the creaking old shed that teemed with life for three or four weeks then settled back, dead quiet, for the rest of the year, with only the wind and ghosts for company.

'We'd call school off for those four weeks.' Nancy's mum had a cheeky glint in her eye. 'See, my mum was my teacher. Once a week my lessons would arrive down our dusty road, tossed off the back of the mail truck. My mum would help me learn spelling and work out my sums. But when shearing time came around, that was it. The lessons stayed on my desk, unopened. I'd take off mustering with my dad. School had to wait till I wasn't busy.

'Between musters, I'd spend my time in the shearing shed. As soon as a shearer finished his sheep, he'd send it down the shute to the pens below. The rouse-about would race to pick up the fleece and fling it out across a huge table to be skirted and classed. Then he'd race back and sweep the boards before the shearer came out with his next sheep to shear. There might be eight or ten shearers going for it at the same time. That rouse-about would be run off his feet, everyone shouting for him. So, I'd grab a broom and help sweep. Alec was my favourite shearer. I always made sure his patch of boards was really clean and clear of wool. He kept lollies for me in his pocket. He reckoned I was the best little rouse-about there ever was.

'At the end of the day, it didn't matter how tired you were,' her mum tells Nancy, 'I'd be there with my dad, counting the sheep out of the pens, then climbing up on Tess, my horse, and tailing a mob back to their home paddock. They looked naked, the sheep, their woolly clothes stripped off, standing there shivering in their lily-white undies. I'd close my eyes to keep the dust out. Then I'd nearly fall out of the saddle, the big orange sun sinking to sleep over my shoulder. Even the flies'd get sleepy on dusk.

'One time, a newborn lamb got left behind. A few lambs were born before shearing that year. In the rush and scramble, going from pen to pen and through the shed, this little one lost its mum. It was hanging way behind when we took the last mob of freshly shorn sheep back to their paddock. Dad and I waited by the gate for ages to see if it would get back together with its mum. Mothering-up we called it. The rest of the mob were taking off, spreading out across the paddock, like balls of cotton wool dotted between the dry brown tufts of grass. This little lamb stood there looking up at us, big eyes, bleating its heart out for its mother. No mother came. The more it bleated, the more I pestered my dad, just like you do.'

'Were you a good pesterer?' Nancy asks, wide-eyed.

'The best!' Her mum screws up her face and makes her voice whine. 'Pretty please, best dad in the world, can we take the little lost lamby home? I'll look after it all on my own, cross my heart and hope to die, and I'll never ask for anything ever again, and you'll be my best friend. Promise.'

'That's pretty good pestering.'

'It must have been, 'cause he gave in. My dad looked big and gruff but he had a heart as soft as marshmallow in hot chocolate.

He bent down and picked up the little wobbly thing, with its tight white curls and big knobbly knees, and tucked it under his strong arm as he climbed back up on his horse. My heart was pounding, thumping ready to burst. A lamb all of my own. I couldn't wait to find a bottle and teat and warm some powdered milk for its first feed. I could be its mum.

'We became best friends, Lambo and me. She followed me everywhere. I'd do my school work out in the garden just so she could join in. She wasn't much good at spelling. Maths was more her thing.'

Nancy giggles.

'When we finished school for the day, Lambo and I would race off and visit our other friends. There was this real turkey who ruled the roost down the chook-yard, and Belle the old sheepdog. She was too slow to go out mustering any more. Belle and Lambo and

I would sit around eating mud-cake, sipping gum-leaf tea, and talking about boyfriends.'

Nancy imagines dressing up for disco parties, practising a dance routine, making up songs . . . with a lamb and a mangy old sheepdog as best friends!

The phone rings but her mum lets the answering machine take a message.

Emails come in, but her mum says they can wait.

A fax arrives and falls on the floor. Her mum just leaves it lying there.

She and Nancy are having too much fun.

Through her mum's workroom window, Nancy watches some fleecy white clouds spreading out across a paddock of sky. Nancy's mum has moved across to the couch. Nancy snuggles in next to her, glad to be mothered-up. Mum holds her close.

'Remember the wool Gran sent you?'

'Yes.'

'Maybe you could ask her to teach you how to spin, next time we visit.'

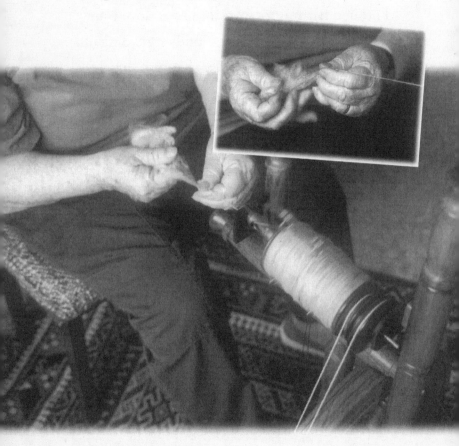

Nancy has the wool safely tucked away in her secret box. She imagines making something special with wool she's spun herself.

'How did sheep get their wool?'

Nancy's mum looks blank.

'Can you tell me a Dreamtime story about sheep?' Nancy asks.

'Maybe Baa Baa Black Sheep?' her mum jokes.

'No, a real one!'

'Well . . . my mum used to tell me stories about the Lamb of God and how the world was made, a bit like Dreamtime stories I suppose. But, see, sheep are newcomers here in Australia. They only arrived a couple of hundred years ago on ships from way over the other side of the world. From places like England and Spain, but Dreamtime characters like the echidna . . .'

'Binggaldamba.' Nancy is quick to chip in.

'. . . have been walking this land for thousands and thousands of years, even long before Gee Whiz was born!'

The late afternoon sun shines through the leaves outside, sending shadows dancing across the wall. Nancy and her mum take their time to cuddle and wonder, making out shapes in the shadow dance.

The light is fading, the sun is sinking, it's nearly night-time. After night comes day, thinks Nancy. That means it's tomorrow.

Tomorrow means school. And school means another day with no Venus Flytrap.

Frantically, Nancy traces fly-paths in the sky, all the way back to the shearing shed and then to her own back yard and the smelly echidna. Back to where she left her excuse as to why she couldn't bring her Venus Flytrap to school.

'Listen to this, Mum, listen. Does this sound better?'

Her mum is still playing with patterns on the wall.

'I can say that the Venus Flytrap was too greedy for its own good. See, Gee reckons that's what happened to the binggaldamba. It was greedy and didn't share, and all those spikes in its back are spears.'

She goes on. 'So, my Flytrap got so greedy it was grabbing flies out of the air. No manners. Just grabbing flies from all over

the world and stuffing them down.
Its eyes were way too big for the size
of its belly. And it didn't share.
It grew bigger and bigger,
fatter and fatter. It grew so big,
and so fat that it . . .

burst

. . . just this morning.
It burst and green
slimy stuff spurted
out everywhere.'
Nancy likes that bit the best. All over her
bedroom window and down the walls, mess
dripping off everything. 'And there were
broken little legs and wings and a few
squashed-up flies' eyes!

'And so, Miss Susan, I'm sorry but there's no Venus Flytrap left for Show and Tell.'

Nancy turns to her mum, proud of her latest story.

'You know, you could just tell Miss Susan the truth, Nance.' Her mum's eyes are warm, her voice dreamy. 'You wanted a Venus Flytrap so badly that you just had to make one up.'

Nancy lies back in her mother's soft arms. 'Yeah ... maybe ...'

That night Gee arrives back with a special parcel from Nanna. Nancy quickly finishes her jobs cleaning up, brushes her teeth and jumps into bed. Her mum and Gee watch while she carefully opens the newspaper wrapping.

The necklace, curled up in a nest of tissues, is more beautiful than she could ever have dreamed. She touches each one of the shiny red seeds and the long thin quills tipped with

black. Nancy tries the necklace on. It fits
perfectly.

She places it carefully beside her bed,
close, gazing at the red seeds and long quills.
Her eyelids start to droop. She struggles to
keep them open.

'And I brought a story back for you.'
Gee's voice blankets her, his hand stroking

her forehead. 'You see, we have two great Creators, great beings that made everything. They're special to us mob. So special we keep most of their story secret. Every so often, we tell a part to someone who needs the story to make them strong. Someone who can carry that story safely in their heart.'

Nancy hears Gee's voice but she can no longer tell if he's there beside her or travelling with her in a dream.

The first ray of light slips through the blinds in Nancy's bedroom. Her eyes flick open. Red seeds. Quills. It's true! The necklace is there beside her.

Carefully, Nancy touches each seed, running her fingers over the quills. Slowly, she puts the necklace around her neck. Then an idea, only a tiny seed of a thought at first, begins to sprout in her mind.

Nancy goes to her secret box. She finds the wool from Gran. She tip-toes into the kitchen. Her mum and Gee are still asleep. She rummages in the bottom drawer and finds a big paper bag. Back in the bedroom, she lays out the wool and the seed pods Gee brought home. A story comes back to her. Did she hear it, or was it a dream about two great Creators and their yams? When she's ready she places the paper bag, full of her most precious things, beside her school bag.

Nancy finds her own clothes, eats her breakfast, makes her bed, even brushes her hair and cleans her teeth without a whinge. She finds the car keys to stop her mum panicking, and they drive to school.

Nancy isn't worried.

They walk into the school yard.

Nancy walks tall.

They climb the stairs to her classroom.

Nancy hangs her school bag on the hook and walks straight into class, the paper bag held tightly in her hand.

Miss Susan greets Nancy with a cheery good morning, looking closely at the paper bag.

Nancy swallows hard, waiting for the words to take shape in her mouth.

'I'm sorry, Miss Susan.'

Nancy falters. More words form.

'The truth is I don't have a Venus Flytrap.'

Nancy looks at her toes. Even they don't look happy.

'Oh dear.' Miss Susan's voice is serious. She bends down next to Nancy.

At least all the other kids can't hear, Nancy thinks.

'Well, I'm glad you told me now. I wondered what the problem was. As it turns out, Hughie brought his.'

Hughie Robertson, the boy six doors down from Nancy who loves Coco Pops with lots of sugar, holds his Venus Flytrap up proudly, smiling at Nancy.

Nancy tries to smile back. She swallows again and tells Miss Susan, 'I do have something else I could share.'

Hughie shows his Venus Flytrap to the class.

He says that you need to keep them wet, and
they like lots of sun, and in warmer parts of
Australia like Brazil they can grow big enough
to eat real people.

The class is amazed.

Miss Susan asks anyone if they know where

Brazil is on the world map. Sarah does, of course. Hughie says he knows Brazil is not in Australia and he never said that anyway.

Miss Susan turns to Nancy.

'And what have you brought in, Nancy?'

Nancy stands up. It seems to take forever to reach the front of the class. Her hand is getting sweaty gripping the paper bag full of seed pods and wool.

Then she is standing there, looking at the rest of the class, their sunflower-faces staring up. She forgets what she wanted to say, then steadies herself and begins.

First, she tells the Story of the Two Yams. She asks her school mates to carry it safely in their hearts.

'Where my Gee comes from, there are two Creators, two brothers. When they walked across the earth, they were huge, like sky-high people.'

She'd practised the story before school.
Gee listened and helped with the bits she
wasn't sure about. Softly to herself, all the way
to school in the car, she went over it again and
again. And she'd practised not speaking the
names of the two great Creators. Not to her
whole class. She pinkie-finger-double-swore
with Gee that she would keep the secrets safe
and know the right time for telling.

'One brother is all serious and works very
hard. He reckons hard work is the thing that
makes you strong. The other brother is playful
and cheeky and plays tricks all the time.
He reckons life is all play. That's why there's
the Story of the Two Yams.'

She can hear Gee's voice speaking through
her. And Nanna's and his aunty's and uncle's
voices through him. And all the other voices
of all the other storytellers.

She goes on with the story, telling how the

serious Creator planted his yam way down deep in the earth.

'If you want to dig it out, it takes a long time and lots of work. But once you pull it up and wash the dirt off, it's ready to eat. It's got lots of things in it that make you strong.

'The cheeky Creator thought that was too much hard work. He just scratched a little hole in the earth and put his yam there so it was easy to get at.

'This time it was the serious, hard-working Creator who played the trick. He quickly found where his brother had planted his yam close to the surface. He did something to it to make it sour.' Nancy explains that this part of the story is only for boys to hear. Gee couldn't tell her what it was that the Creator did to make his brother's yam sour.

'That's secret,' she says.

Some boys up the back of the class smother a giggle, as if they already know.

A ripple of excitement scuds across the class. Everyone is busy imagining what could have happened to the yam to make it sour. Nancy waits till they grow quiet again and listen. Then she carries on, working hard to get each detail right.

'So, even though the cheeky Creator's yam is easy to get, you can't eat it straight away. You have to wrap that yam up in bark and hit it with a rock and soak it in water for more than a day till all the poisons leave.

'But with the yam that is buried deep in the earth, even though you have to work really hard, when you get that yam up you can eat it straight away.'

Everyone in the room is very quiet.

Nancy passes the seed pods around. There's enough for everyone in the class to share. She shows them how to peel back the dry pod, collect the yellowy seeds and wait for them to turn orange then red. She explains how you have to be patient till they are just turning before you drill a hole through them for making beads. If you miss the right moment, they get too hard and you've got no beads to thread.

Then she passes around pieces of wool from her Gran for everyone to feel. Next time she goes to her Gran's place, she's going to spin enough wool to make her own beanie and see if she can thread it with red seeds.

'That wool comes from where my mum grew up. There were that many flies out there, they used to get in her eyes and her ears and even up her nose. She swallowed a whole mouthful of flies one day. She did. True.'

A few of the class splutter, others doubt it could be true, calling out to Miss Susan that you'd die if that was true.

'But listen to this.' Nancy gathers them back in before the whole mob breaks loose and chatters wildly. 'Her dad said not to worry.' She pauses. All eyes and ears are back with her. 'Her dad told her, "Just blow your nose." Sure enough, she blew and the whole lot came flying back out!'

The whole class falls about laughing.

Miss Susan thanks Nancy for her yam story,
which is very interesting for their study of
plants, she says. As for the flies out the nose?
The class will have to wait for the lesson on
the Human Body to find out about that.
They might be surprised about the mouth
and the nose, she tells them.

Nancy can see Miss Susan's smile touching
them—Hughie and each of them in turn.

Nancy feels the wool and the beads in her hand and feels a glow like the morning sun. But the glow Nancy feels this time is coming from the very centre of herself.

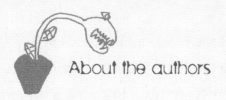

About the authors

Meme McDonald's family is from Western Queensland. Meme writes books for children and adults. Her first book, *Put Your Whole Self In*, won the 1993 Braille and Talking Book Award. The animation of her second book, *The Way of the Birds*, was nominated for an AFI Award and won a best-film award at the Cinanima Festival in Portugal.

Boori Monty Pryor's family is from North Queensland. His mother's people are Kunggandji and his father is from the Birra-gubba Nation. Boori is a performer, storyteller and didjeridoo player. In 1993 he received an award for the Promotion of Indigenous Culture from the National Aboriginal Islander Observance Committee.

The first book Meme McDonald and Boori Pryor wrote together was *Maybe Tomorrow*. *My Girragundji* won the 1999 CBC of Australia Award for Younger Readers; *The Binna Binna Man* was the winner of the Ethel Turner Prize for Young People's Literature, the Ethnic Affairs Commission Award, and Book of the Year in the 2000 NSW Premier's Literary Awards. Boori's narration of *My Girragundji* and *The Binna Binna Man* won the Australian Audio Book of the Year Award. The third book about the same boy, *Njunjul the Sun*, was published in 2002.

Acknowledgements

The idea for *Flytrap* began when Agnes Nieuwenhuizen asked for a 'tall tale' to be told for a literary dinner organised by the Australian Centre for Youth Literature. Erica Wagner was in the audience, and she suggested the 'tall tale' could become a book.

Our deepest thanks to Grace Lovell for inspiring the 'tall tale', and for her editorial comment as her story grew into this book.

Thanks to Aunty Val Stanley for guiding our understanding of stories and when and how to tell them; to Aunty Alma Fourmile for telling 'The Story of the Two Yams'; and to cousin Gerry Fourmile for sharing his knowledge.

We are very grateful to our mothers, who each gave of themselves to the book, trusting in us as writers.

And many thanks to the friends who waded through early drafts and remained encouraging, particularly Jodi Satya for her insight and suggestions.

Many thanks to the teachers at Clifton Hill Primary School—Peta Hirschfeld, Susan Butler and Toni Hanns—for the time they set aside. And thanks to the Grade Three students for their response to the manuscript and eagerness in front of the camera: Anna and Josh Debinski, Alice Debney, Greta Ferguson, Maddy Foote, Madeleine Hawkins, Sandi Ieraci, Phoebe Imms, Oliver Jach, Nicole Johnson, Jake Jones, Sophie

Karagiannidis, Anna Kilpatrick, Jane Kingsford, Julian La Rosa, Zac Matthews, Sarah McKechnie, John Panagopoulos, Yoti Pechlivanidis, Jessica Stagnitta, Hugh Steele, Ahliah Tilley and Nicholas Velevski.

A special thanks to our neighbour Hugo Roberts for his enthusiasm while being photographed; to Spike for putting up with it; to Sharyn Prentice and Paul Ket for horses and dogs and opinions on things; and to Anne White for dusting off the spinning wheel.

This book, along with many others, owes a great deal to Ruth Grüner for her flexibility and imagination, making words and photographs come to life as design. We thank her for her inspired work.

Thanks to cousin Lillian Fourmile for her great talent as a painter, and for the work she so generously made available to our books. Thanks to Harry Todd for his drawings, his hard work, and for being a great nephew.

Above all we give thanks to Allen & Unwin for their belief in our writing. Thanks to Rosalind Price and Sue Flockhart, who gave the manuscript the care and attention it needed to become whole. Thanks to Karin Riederer for promoting our work, and to the marketers, designers and booksellers who enthuse others to read the books.

Our thanks to Jenny Darling and Jacinta Di Mase, for guiding our work, to Young Australia Workshop for their ongoing support, and to Lesley Reece and Natasha Roe, as always.

website: **www.mememcdonald.com**